Will Dillman

Across the Wheat

Will Dillman

Across the Wheat

ISBN/EAN: 9783743418530

Manufactured in Europe, USA, Canada, Australia, Japa

Cover: Foto ©Andreas Hilbeck / pixelio.de

Manufactured and distributed by brebook publishing software
(www.brebook.com)

Will Dillman

Across the Wheat

ACROSS THE WHEAT

BY WILL DILLMAN

––––––––

REVILLO, S. D.
THE ITEM
1898

TO VINA

And Dora took the child, and went her way
Across the wheat......
                              The reapers reap'd,
And the sun fell, and all the land was dark.

                                        TENNYSON.

CONTENTS

CONTENTS

ISADORE

IN the middle of the wheat, where the south winds, slow or
  fleet,
Bore a fragrance from the prairies of the roses, faint and
  sweet,
There the nestlings piped and peeped where the gray-brown
  stones were heaped,
Where the plowshare never troubled, where the reaper never reaped.

In the weird and stilly noon of the nights of waning June,
When the fields were sleeping 'neath the yellow halo of the
  moon,
Dreamfully the barefoot child strayed among the roses wild,
Thro' the dewy hollows, pausing where the mossy stones were
  piled.

O, the little wand'ring feet, wending thro' the bending wheat;
O, the childhood gone forever; O, the years so cruel, fleet!
Listen to the homely lore pitying midnight spirits bore;
As the childish watcher heard it, hear the tale of Isadore.

I.

In the seasons past and gone dwelt two brothers, Frank and
  John,
By the ever stretching prairie countless cattle roamed upon;
In a simple, strong abode, builded by the winding road,
By the rippled rapid river where the turbid waters flowed.

Frank was weaker of the twain, for a grim disease amain
Thro' the years had racked his body, leaving still a cloudless
    brain.
John was tall and brownly tanned, mighty-armed and strong
    of hand;
And his limbs were sturdy, treading fall by fall the furrowed
    land.

Now the brothers spoke no more as they used in time before,
When they wrought or when they rested, of the lovely Isa-
    dore.
For in either's heart, alone and deep hidden. there had grown
For the girl a silent passion but to mutest lovers known.

Busy seasons gliding fast, now were youth and boyhood past;
And the brothers came to manhood's grave and sterner years
    at last.
Now their parents. bent and gray and o'er-wrought. had pas-
    sed away;
Alone they sowed and reaped and watched the herd. as farm-
    ers may.

All a brother's love they bore for each other; but a more
Sacred passion grew within them for the queenly Isadore.
Each was hoping thro' the years. hoping still 'neath doubts
    and tears.
That he might at some day claim her. know her joys and share
    her tears.

Now one late and autumn night the wild storm was at its
    height;
Only in the old farm kitchen burned the wood-fire. warm and
    bright.

There the brothers lingered still near the midnight hour; and
shrill
Raged the tempest; and the farm-house shook and shuddered,
roof and sill.

Thus spoke John, and looked away to the window, "Frank, all
day
I have tried to tell this secret; listen, then, to what I say:
When the winter days are o'er, and the flowers bloom once
more,
This old house will bloom with sunshine and the smiles of Isadore."

As one standing 'neath the bud of the hawthorne hears the
thud
Of the first clods on the coffin of the nearest of his blood,
So upon the brother's ears fell the name that all the years
He had loved to whisper nightly 'neath the dim unnumbered
spheres.

Yet he silent sat, and raised not his head, but like one dazed
At the slowly glowing embers with unchanging eyelids gazed.
Then upon a sudden fell from his soul the binding spell;
And he seized the honest brown hand, saying, "Brother, it is
well."

On a bright and joyous day in the mating time of May,
When winds were hushed, and all the plain a waveless ocean
lay,
Under apple blossoms hour John the sturdy farmer bore
To his home the happy maiden, bore the queenly Isadore.

Frank the brother stood beside the old door-way, on the wide
Spreading porch and, hands extended, welcomed home the
  groom and bride.
No one seeing him might know that beneath this smiling show
Beat a heart all crushed and shattered by a single mighty
  blow.

II.

Thro' the villages and farms rose and rumbled War's alarms:
And threat'ning drums and stirring trumpets called, "To
  arms! to arms!"
Many a brave and noble band quit its forges, quit its land;
Many a home was left unguarded by a strong and manly hand.

At the cottage door the three stood and parted—(Far and free
On the morning air was borne the war-drum's dreadful re-
  veille!)—
John the manly brave and true in his uniform of blue,
Isadore the young and tearful, Frank beside the silent two.

While the birds of morning passed thro' the dewy boughs, and
  fast
Fell the girlish tears, the husband held her, kissed her for the
  last.
So the soldier left her there with the sunlight on her hair,
Saying, "Frank, protect and guard her; Frank, I leave her in
  your care."

Down the winding road he passed, while the heavy musket
  cast

On his manly shoulder glistened, gleamed and glistened to the
last.
On the farthest hill he stood, looking backward while he
could;
Saw the cattle in the farm-yard; saw the green and pleasant
wood;

Saw the farm-house white and fair; saw the still and lonely
pair,
The patient yielding brother and the young wife standing
there.
Burning tears unheeded flowed down the soldier's cheeks; he
strode,
Leaving all things dear behind him, down the long and winding road.

So the soldier went; and still watched the lonely two, until
The figure small and smaller grew, and vanished o'er the hill.
Then the silent brother turned to his fields, for he discerned
A profound and sacred sorrow on the face of her who yearned.

And the lonely Isadore, fairer, queenlier than before,
"He is gone," she stood repeating, "he is gone," and evermore,
While the sunny day wore on, and she turned herself anon
To her household cares, she murmured, ever murmured, "he
is gone."

III.

O, the long and lonely years, time of mingled hopes and fears:
O, the eyes grown dim with watching; O, the silent flowing
tears!

All alone with thoughtful brow wrought the old man at the
    plow;
All his boys had gone to battle; two had perished bravely now.

And the mother at the gate wandered down to watch and wait,
While the evening shadows lengthened, while the hour was
    growing late.
And the young babe grown apace had forgot his father's face,
And marked no more the stillness and the ever vacant place.

And the children 'round the door played in silence evermore,
For a shadow like the shadow of a dark cloud hovered o'er.
Nightly down the yellow road where the summer moonlight
    flowed,
Peered the maiden: there he vanished, glancing backward as
    he strode.

Now the blue-eyed Isadore stiller grew, and sang no more
At her house-work, and her wistful eyes were sadder than be-
    fore.
And the brother, strong above all the griefs he suffered of,
Ever sought to cheer her, patient in his silent sinless love.

Now the time of yellow shocks came again; and crying flocks
Soared above, and in the sunshine crew the faint and distant
    cocks.
In the evening Frank returned with his horses, and discerned
Thro' the door the young wife standing where the twilight
    embers burned.

At the evening meal the two sat in silence. Faintly thro'
Door and window came the lonely chirp of crickets in the dew.

Now the cheerful farmer Brown, home returning from the
    town
With the newest tidings, entered, stood in silence, looking
    down.

While the stricken Isadore looked upon him, lo, a more
Deathly pallor came upon her, spread her cheeks and fore-
    head o'er.
To the kindly man she fled wild and helpless, "Speak!" she
    said,
"Is he killed? Ah heaven, I know it! Tell me! Speak man!
    Is he dead?"

"Yes, my girl." And Isadore heard no word of tidings more.
For the pitying farmer caught her falling swooning to the
    floor.
Tenderly they laid her down on the couch; and farmer Brown
Brought his kind old wife to tend her, and a doctor from the
    town.

IV.

Over sanded roads and gray John the soldier marched away
With his comrades, passing cornfields, passing meadows sweet
    with hay;
During all his weary tramps thinking still of her, in camps
Of the South, in midnight watches, in the lonely dews and
    damps.

So by one and one were gone dark and cruel years; and John
With his comrades marched and fought: and yet the bloody
    War went on.

In the battle's smoke and roar, on the marches, or when o'er
Silent tents the moon hung watching, still he dreamt of Isa-
    dore.

Now in autumn time was made yet a fiercer battle. Blade
Clashed on bloody blade, and banners waved, and ranks were
    lowly laid.
Long the soldier fought and well where his comrades reeled
    and fell,
Where the screeching shells were hottest, in the battle's red-
    dest hell.

In a charge too rashly fought John and all his line were
    caught
From their comrades, and as captives to the dreaded prison
    brought.
And the tearful message, read in his native village, said
These were killed and these were wounded, naming John
    among the dead.

Many months he languished there in the filthy prison, where
Sickened comrades lay about him, squalor filling earth and
    air.
Frightful months the soldier passed in the ghastly prison
    cast;
But deliv'rance and the flag he loved and bled for came at
    last.

Now the cruel course was run; now were furled and folded,
    one
After one, the shell-torn banners; now the awful War was
    done.

Now the soldiers, sick and sore, thought to wander home once
    more,
Thought again to see the farm-house with the loved ones at
    the door.

V.

In the summer night the sweet grass was crushed beneath
    the feet
Of the homeward plodding soldier, as he passed the fragrant
    wheat.
Now were all his labors o'er, thus he thought, and evermore
Would he dwell in peace and quiet with the love of Isadore.

So the weary man, elate with sweet visions, could not wait,
But plodded, plodded onward till he reached the farm-house
    gate.
Joyous tears, the least like those he had shed at parting, rose
To the weary soldier's eyelids as he neared his journey's
    close.

Thro' the somber summer night from the window gleamed a
    light.
Coming near, he looked within, and moaned in sorrow at the
    sight.
For he saw his Isadore lying still and pale, and o'er
Snowy cheek and pillow streamed her hair as golden as of
    yore.

Near the couch of spotless down sat wife of farmer Brown,
With her kindly eyes and features and her quaint and ample
    gown.

As she stroked in mother's wise all the flowing hair, the eyes
Opened, gazing far and wistful, as on cloudless summer skies.

Kneeling trembling on the floor, now the soldier held once
    more
In his arms the pale-cheeked woman, held the happy Isadore.
All her sorrow vanished when once again he held her; then
Was she silent, saying only, "John, I dreamt you came again."

Frank the silent brother came thro' the doorway, with the
    same
Patient face that hinted not a silent love's undying flame.
While the soldier held her fast in his trembling arms, she
    passed
From earth's longings, ever smiling, ever happy to the last.

And the brothers by the bed gazed upon the sinless dead,
One the loved and one the loving, and no single word they
    said.
And the curling hair of gold lay about the forehead cold ;
And the brief young life was compassed, as a story that is
    told.

In the middle of the wheat, there they laid her, where the
    fleet
South winds ever bear a fragrance of the roses, faint and
    sweet.
There the nestlings pipe and peep, where the stones their vig-
    il keep,
Where the plowshare never troubles, where the reapers never
    reap.

IN THE JIM VALLEY

They're a-harvestin' the wheatfields in the Valley of the Jim;
I can hear the reapers clatter, soundin' kind of low an' dim;
See the yello' fields a-wavin', an' the shocks in crooked rows:
An' house an' barn, an' mother out a-hengin' up the clo'es:
See the cattle in the pastur', an' the ol' gray limpin' mule;
An' the yello' heifer standin' in the water keepin' cool.
An' I try to fight again' it as a sort of silly whim,
But I wisht 'at I was back there in the Valley of the Jim.

Now it's fall, an' they're a-thrashin' an' a-plowin' up the
    ground;
An' the air is sort of hazy, an' the gulls are sailin' 'round.
An' the sun looks kind of yello' in the smoky afternoon;
An' at ev'ning you can listen to the steamer's sleepy tune.
See the horses comin' home f'om work, an' smell their sweaty
    coats;
Hear 'um smashin' through the stubble, tired an' hungry for
    their oats.
Now it's growin' sort of dusky, an' they're doin' up the chores.
An' the kitchen fire is burnin', an' it's chilly out o' doors.
I can smell the eggs an' coffee, an' I know my little trim
Lovin' mother's gettin' supper in the Valley of the Jim.

Onc't I had a elder brother in the Valley of the Jim,
An' he was a homely fello', an' I ust to go with him
To the pastur' for the cattle, an' a-fishin', an' around:
'N I mind he ust to carry me acrost the stubble ground.

An' we ust to sit a-fishin' of a summer afternoon
By the crick, an' hear the gophers chirp, an' listen to the tune
Of the bobolink an' blackbird.—O I recollect it well.—
An' we liked the sleepy water, an' the sort o' fishy smell
Of the ol' dry bank, with craw-fish bones an' clam-shells lay-
    in' there;
An' we'd hear the dreamy cryin' of the plover in the air.

An' then one day in fall they buried him on father's hill;
'N I cried all day, an' wished 'at I was laid along of Bill.
For it seemed so queer an' lonesome 'thout no brother any
    more.—
An' now the grass is dyin' there, an' winds are sighin' o'er.
I can hear the sor'ful meado' lark a-singin' over him.—
O I wisht 'at I was back there in the Valley of the Jim.

"WHEN YOND' SAME STAR."

"When yond' same star that's westward from the pole"
Glowed in the dark-blue space thus over-bright,
And the winds kept the silent sleep of night,
By the still lake we rested from our stroll.

O I do mind your hair's abundantness
When yonder star was westward from the pole.
I mind the faint and sweetest scent that stole
From countless silken foldings of your dress.

I wonder, does that white contented swan
Still dip and frolic where the ripples roll,
When yonder star is westward from the pole?
I wonder, does that fountain murmur on?

So often as I wonder with my soul,
As now, where pulseless midnight hushes are,
I think of you, I long for you afar,
When yonder star is westward from the pole.

OLD BILL WILLIAMS

Where that old sod shanty is,
  Old Bill Williams, he lived there.
He got froze to death; that's his
  Grave out by the plowing, where
All the sun-flow'rs are. He came
  To this country—I don' know—
From Vermont—an' took that claim.
  Maybe twenty years ago.

Well, one time the boy an' him
  Got caught out; an' I suppose
He wrapped all his clo'es on Jim,
  An' laid down with him, an' froze.
That's the way we found 'um, Bill
  Dead, an' Jim all right, an' so,
Never missed 'im gretly, still
  Boys felt kind o' sorry though.

WHEN JENNIE PASSED

There was a minute's silence in the crowd.
Old Silas drew his feet up under him.
Young Daily sighed and frowned and breathed less loud.
    Bill Hawkins leered upon her with a grim
Bad smile, and turned and spat the other way.
    Great guilty heads were bent, and glances cast
From corners of men's eyes, and hearts that day
    Had higher better thoughts, when Jennie passed.

Young Williams stood with folded arms, erect.
    He did not mingle with the village men.
He raised his hat; he saw her face, sun-flecked
    And fair; he caught a faint perfume; and when
Her glance met his with modest sweet surprise,
    His heart stood still, fell, rose, beat high and fast.
The corner sign-board danced before his eyes,
    And all was dizziness, when Jennie passed.

YENNIE

Ay ben setten har des efning en mæ lettle lunesome place,
   Un da lunesome clock ben ticken on da shulf.
Ay ben tenken bote von lettle soony headt un preety face.
   Ay ben sadt unt lunesome too tonate mæsulf.

Efryting hæ ben so qviet ulmos' ay ben 'fraid to mofe,
   Oonly ven ay vapen tear ofe mit mæ slief.
Un mæ doge ben looken at me, setten qviet bæ da stofe:
   Poor ool' Roover, hæ ben lunesome too, ay b'lief.

Poor ool' Roover, never you vont yump mit her un play some
      more;
   Never run un meet her ven she com en sate;
Never you vont leek her lettle handt ven she com troo da door,
   Fore dose lettle handts ben gone avay tonate.

Many jears ago her mooder dæ, ven ve ben 'cross da sea;
   Yennie ben da oonly shiidrens vot ve haf.
She ben looken lak her mooder ven she setten on mæ knee;
   Ay ben tinken bote her mooder ven she laf.

Ay ben valken troo da pesture var she juse to drave da cowse,
   Un dey lift dar headt op ven ay com alonge;
Un dey looken longe tem at mæ ven ay goen to da hoose,
   Lak dey vonder var poor lettle Yennie gone.

Un her hat un sholl ben hengen on da nail behande da door,
   Unt her lettle shoose, un dress so clean un vate. - -

Never she vont need dose lettle shoose to put on any more,
Fore dose lettle feet ben gone avay tonate.

Lettle Yennie, lettle Yennie, vot for do you die so soon?
Oll da nebber boyse un girlse dey lofe you too.
Efry tem you haf da deener ven ay comen home bae noon,
Oo mæ Yennie, ay skel bæ so lunesome noo!

Lettle Yennie, lettle Yennie, oolvis ben so sveet un goode:
Oolvis doen op da vork, un sing un laf.
Noo ay got von lettle grafe doon bæ da corner of da rude,
Unt von lettle shoose un hat, dos oll ay haf.

Poor ool' Roover, never you vont yump mit her un play some
    more;
  Never run unt meet her ven she com en sate;
Never you vont leek her lettle handt ven she com troo da
    door,
  Fore dose lettle handts ben gone avay tonate.

BALLAD OF BAILEY'S RIG

In the early light we set, while the frost was lying yet
  White and clean—we'd pulled from Hull's night before.
And by sun-up or about we had half a setting out,
  And the old thing chewing wheat, howl and roar.

Then the wind rose in the south, high and hotter. Woman's
  mouth
  Full of hair and bunnit strings as she run
With a ca'f and wotter pail tacking up against the gale.
  And we worked and sweat and swore in the sun.

Bailey standing on the top by the pile of sieves would mop
  Out his eyes and watch the cloud rolling near,
Till a scorching headfire broke through the marsh with flame
  and smoke.—
  And he waved to Jerry Hicks, engineer.

"Stop 'er! Run 'er 'round!" says 'e. "What a cussed fool I be
  Not to know the lake was dry, and the crick.
Back 'er up! Pull out o' here! Or we'll lose three thousand
  clear!
  Make the plowing if you never strike a lick!"

Engine backed in with a twist while the sizzing spigots hissed.
  Black-red smoke a-booming on straight across.
Jerry started with a jerk. "Pull 'er open! Make 'er work!
  Throw the gov'ner belt to hell!" yelled the boss.

How he made her jump and bound! How she climbed across
    the ground!
  And the fireman stuffing straw fit to kill.
And the pitchers sitting blind with the smoke and dirt behind.
  And we sailed across the field, down the hill.

Boiler hot and popping steam. Bailey letting loose a stream
  From the oil-can on the straw. Forty rods!
Jerry steering past the rocks tried the fiery-hissing cocks.
  "Bill, her wotter's getting low, by the gods!"

Tried the pump. It wouldn't go. Tried the hot injector. No.
  "Run 'er dry then!" Bailey yelled. "Make 'er dig!"
Close behind the header blew red-hot cinders on the crew.
  And we made the plowing safe with the rig.

THE FARMER OF THE PRAIRIES

The farmer of the prairies trod with slow,
    Tired steps at evening, when his toil was done.
To'rd his poor house. Far in the west a glow
    Was waning where had sunk the autumn sun.

He sank upon the wooden steps, and drew
    His plow shoes from his swelled and heavy feet.
He bared his massive brow. A warm wind blew.
    Bringing a restful fragrance, faint and sweet.

The furrowed fields lay dark and silent. Now
    A dog barked on with tireless energy.
Faint, far away, a neighbor's lonely cow
    Bawled, and a wagon rattled distantly.

Long, long the farmer sat unmoving there.
    His whiskered cheek upon his hand, the kind
Wind toying with his gray and moistened hair.
    His eyes unseeing, fixed. And now behind

The shuddering, solemn corn the moon arose.
    Long, long he thought upon his wasted life,
Its years of useless toil. He thought of those
    He loved, his absent boys, his buried wife.

*   *   *   *   *   *

Late, late it grows. The last sad cricket's call

Has ceased; and in the moon's pale silver glare
The commonplace has seemed to vanish, all.
I see a tragic figure sitting there.

SENCE NELLIE'S MOVED AWAY

Some afternoons I let the cattle feed down here,
To'rds the old house where Nellie ust to live.   It's kind of
     queer.
They ain't no flow'rs ner curtains, and a glass is busted out,
An' weeds is growin' in the little path.   It's been about
Three weeks I guess, er mebbe four, sence Nellie's moved
     away.
Sometimes I let 'um feed down here, along to'rds evening, say.

O' course now I don't s'pose 'at Nellie 'd ever think of me.
She's gone off there to Illinois er somewheres.   Still now she
Would often stop an' talk to me—An' now it's summer time.
An' everthing is hot an' dry, an' Nellie's gone, an' I'm—
I s'pose I'm kind of foolish—yup—but I can't help 'ut say
I'm lonesome like sence Nellie's moved away.

I recollect that afternoon she come an' told me,   "Fred,"
She says, "we're go'n' away f'om here," an' stood an' hung 'er
     head.
I see the wind an' sunshine playin' with 'er hair, an' then
My throat stuck an' I couldn't speak, an' she walked home
     again.
I wisht I could of thought o' some few words er so to say.
I've thought o' lots sence Nellie's moved away.

Oh the days is long an' sultry fer a fello' now like me,
'At ain't got nothin' much to do but herdin' princip'ly.

Right here's the place I hold 'er hand that day a little while.
I wonder now if she was mad?   An' yet I seen 'er smile.
I wisht she hadn't gone.   I wisht she'd come again an' stay.
I feel so sad sence Nellie's moved away.

AFTER THE CURTAIN DROPS

We gaze entranced upon the shifting stage.
  Where stride the players in the tragedy,
And tremble at the Moor's majestic rage,
  And shudder at Iago's treachery,
And weep for Desdemona's cruel death,
  But when at last the wondrous drama stops,
We brush away the tears with freer breath,
  And turn to action, when the curtain drops.
    After the many parts are played,
      After the music stops,
    After the exits all are made,
      After the curtain drops.

My friends will pause and sigh some little space,
  And here and there, perchance, a tear may fall,
And many men will look upon my face,
  Serene and cold, and deem that after all
I'm better off.   And they will make for me
  A grave somewhere among the clover tops,
And one poor girl, perhaps, will come and see,
  And weep and pity, when the curtain drops.
    After the striving ends at last,
      After the struggle stops,
    After the heart aches all are past,
      After the curtain drops.

WHEN WINTER'S COMIN' ON

Oh a fello' feels so cheerful-like some days,
When the prairie grass is withered, and you dig potatœs, say;
And the geese and ducks are leavin', and the sky is cold an'
    gray;
And the fodder rasps an' rustles where it lays.

You feel a sort of sorro' for the summer time that's gone;
But there's a kind of happy feelin' though,
When you know the fall is passin' and the winter's comin' on.
And you hear the autumn winds a-sighin' so.

You see your woman takin' in the clo'es,
Er a-workin' 'round the shanty, and you feel a happy thrill
When you think you might 'a' lost 'er and you've got 'er with
    you still.
Oh a fello' feels so thankful days like those.

RAIN IN HARVEST

At two the white-hot sun was overcast
With shreds of pale gray mist;
And in the vast
And reaching west deep banks arose,
Cool-blue and amethyst.

With far, faint blows,
Tap, tap, and tap, the farm mechanic hammered.
The somber crows
Flapped gloomily from hill to hill.
By still,
Unrippled ponds the scolding blackbird clamored.

Still clanged the reapers o'er the ripened plain,
Distant, and near,
Low and sullen, or loud and clear.

Then came the rain,
Gentle and soft upon the brittle grain.
Upon the long brown leaves,
Upon the yellow shocks,
Upon the fallen sheaves;
Lulling and fresh and cool,
Stilling the farmyard cocks.

Dark'ning the wayside pool.

The drivers hastened home with their teams;
The reapers were left by the wheat.
O welcome rain, how sweet,
How restful and soothing it seems;
O beautiful harvest rain,
After the days of heat,
After the toil and pain.

BALLAD OF NELLIE HANKS

Daylight when I got to town. Roused the doctor out.
  Told him Nellie Hanks was worse; wanted he should go.
Watched my smokin' horses snort clouds of steam about,
  After seven miles of ice, seven miles of snow.

Seen an engine with a car sizzin', creakin past,
  An' a brakeman froze to death, wavin', signalin'.
Got the doctor bundled up on the seat at last,
  Pulled the lines up tight an' whang, off we went agin.

Past the stores an' opree house, past a church an' school,
  'Crost the river where the black steamin' wotter flowed,
Sun most risin' in the east, mornin' sharp an' cool,
  Past the courthouse and the jail, struck the country road.

Horses wild to go ahead, so I let 'um scoot,
  Struck a swift and stiddy trot, tried to hold 'um so.
'Crost the bridges and the pikes, ruts an' holes to boot.
  Seven miles of icy road, seven miles of snow.

But I knowed my jumper'd stood more 'un that before.
  Horses slingin' cannon balls past the doctor's ear.
How we flopped an' banged about. How we ripped an' tore.
  How the doctor clung to me like a drowndin' steer.

"Man," sez he, "for heaven's sake, all my teeth are jes'
  Droppin' out; and all my tools will be lost; and where
Will my cussid bottles be?" "Can't help that," I sez,
  "Nellie Hanks is sick, an' I'll try and git you there."

Down the hills an' 'crost the flats, on through Jones's Gap.
  Neighbors rushin' out the doors, wild to see us go.
Lost a blankit and a quilt, doctor lost 'is cap.
  Seven miles of ice an' ruts, seven miles of snow.

Up through Hanks's trees we rushed, plungin' 'crost the
      banks;
  'Round the haystack and the barn, knockin' down a cow.
Landed at the kitchen door. "My," sez Mrs. Hanks,
  "Sorry that you've hurried so, Nellie's better now."

AUTUMN STORM

Rain in evening. Rain in the early fall.
The cold few drops set in with gathering dusk.
Borne o'er the prairies on the chilling winds
From the vast Rockies. Rain and closing night.

O cold and driving drizzly autumn storm!
It will o'ertake the hastening bier home.
It will pursue the homeward drifting sheep.
The shrinking herd shall flee with lowered heads.
The withered grass of untrod endless plains
Drenched by this storm shall writhe beneath the clouds.

O'er all the vast and gloomy plain tonight
The cold bleak rain is driving. In his tent
The sleeper feels the stray drops on his face.
And sighs from comfort. 'Round the kitchen fire
The sleepy children linger, while the wife
Adjusts the clashing dishes. In the barn
The lantern gleams upon the yellow straw
Under the horses' feet, upon the pegs
Laden with harness, on the farmer's bent
And shadowed form, passing among his steeds.

O happy ye who, blessed with home and friends.

Abide this night against your cheerful fires.
Ye hear the wild storm pelting at the panes.
Ye see your children's faces in the fire light.
Do ye remember us who homelessly
Wander like broken Lear upon the heath?

THE SHANTY ON THE CLAIM

I'm sick and tired of city life. I want to start today,
And git back where Dakoty is, and throw these things away.
And git my old blue overhauls and wommus on agin,
An' stand aside the pastur' when the cows are comin' in.

I want to kiss my mother w'en she meets me at the door,
And see the happy tears a-starting in her eyes once more.
I want to see if father's changed, er if he's jest the same.
I want to eat my supper in the shanty on the claim.

I watch the sun at evening as it kind of sadly drops
In a bank of smoke that raises from a thousand chimbly tops.
And I know the sun is setting clear an' beautiful out there.
Where the meado' lark is singin' on the corner post, an' where

My brothers are a-doing chores and whisteling, and pap's
A-coming from the stable with his milkin' pail perhaps,
And mebbe mother's standing in the door, and O I'm blame
Lonesome when I think about 'um and the shanty on the
     claim.

I'm tired of all these city airs, and all this noise an' din.
I want to see the prairie and the wavin' wheat agin;

And lay down in the cornfield where the wottermelons be,
And watch the sky, and hear the corn a-rasping over me.

I want to go to Hicks's where the dancing is, an' feel
The roarin' inspiration of the old Virginy reel.
I want to waltz with Nellie once agin, and hear 'er say
In a whisper that she likes me, while the screeching fiddles
    play.

I want to go with mother where my little sister lays;
Where the golden-rod is bloomin' through the smoky autumn
    days,
And a kind of gentle sadness seems a-floating in the air.
I want to help my mother tend the flowers we planted
    there......

BED TIME

"Boys, come in and go to bed."
That's what father always said.
In the summer evenings—oh
I guess that was years ago.

When the twilight had about
Faded, and the stars came out.
And we sat and listened to
Insect voices from the dew.

Or a lonely frog, or low
Twitter of a bird or so,
Or a night hawk overhead:
"Boys, come in and go to bed."

Maybe we'll get back some day
To the old farm. Anyway
I'd enjoy it, wouldn't you?
Sit there as we used to do,

On the rough old porch; and then
Try to hear that voice again,
Calling to us from the dead:
"Boys, come in and go to bed."

FLORENCE

I.

It was springtime in Dakota; and the motionless, wide plain
Smiled to welcome back the south winds and the sunny days
again.

Sounds of jocund toil resounded; and the farmers were afield
With their teams and harrows, sowing for the summer's gold-
en yield.

All was filled with exultation at the glad return of spring.
Every creature seemed rejoicing in a new awakening.

Herds of aimless cattle wandered where a tinge of faintest
green
Appearing on the burned and blackened prairie could be seen.

The timid gopher ventured from his winter domicile.
The wild cock boomed at morning from behind the distant
hill.

All day the lark was singing his glad song of joy and love.
The cranes would cry at noonday as they floated high above.

At sunset time the rapid ducks flocked by with whirring
flight.
Afar the geese would sail and soar, and vanish in the night.

Silent evening, solemn evening: just the stars were in the sky,
For the moon was late, and only faintest winds went sighing
by.

But the wakeful frogs were croaking in the marsh, now low,
now higher;
And upon the dim horizon burned a languid prairie fire.

Home returning from the party, Walter Gray and Florence
Lee—
Pretty blue-eyed Florence, fairest one of all the girls was
she—

Home returning in the evening, walking arm in arm were
they,
Softly talking to each other, Florence Lee and Walter Gray.

"Are you sorry? Tell me, Florence," said the manly Walter
Gray.
Then said Florence, "You'll forget me, Walter, when you go
away."

And her voice was sad—she loved him, foolish, timid Florence
Lee—
"You'll find a prettier sweetheart there, and never think of
me."

He stooped and kissed her flushing cheek and warm and girlish brow.
Silent evening, solemn evening; and the moon had risen now.

II.

It was summer in Dakota; and the fields of waving grain
Stretched in endless undulation far across the yellow plain.

Day by day the sun was shining; not a cloud was in the sky.
The wind was still, and only spiders' webs went sailing by.

The pool was green and stagnant where the cattle came to
    drink.
The locust chirped and chattered in the hot grass by the
    brink.

The song birds all were silent; not a note was in the air.
Only humming, dreamy insects broke the stillness every-
    where.

All was wheat: the great sun shone on miles of wheat; the
    scented heat
Smelt of wheat; the gopher chirped of wheat; the blackbird
    screamed of wheat.

And now the grain was ripened, and the harvest was begun.
A thousand men and horses toiled beneath the burning sun.

A thousand reapers clattered thro' the yellow, brittle grain.
All was hurry and excitement o'er the busy, sounding plain.

Sunday came and brought no respite. All the golden sabbath
    day
Toiled the worn-out men and horses, many dropping by the
    way.

Years had passed, and pretty Florence was a fair young
    woman now.
The farm hand's life seemed brighter when she passed him at
    the plow.

The young man's blood would tingle, and his heart would
    leap, perchance,
To catch her glance or clasp her for a moment in the dance.

But hers was such a heart as loves but once, and cannot
    choose.
If it win 'tis filled with gladness, or is shattered if it lose.

When she closed her eyes she saw him; in her dreams she
    heard his voice;
And her heart would droop with sadness, or exult with name
    less joys.

From her father's house came Florence with her empty water
    pail;
Stopped beside the meadow pasture, stood and leaned upon
    rail.

It was sunset, radiant sunset; from the meadow came the
    sound
Of the home-returning cattle, treading o'er the hollow ground.

In the fields the reapers clattered high and lower, and anon
Came the cries of weary drivers as they urged their horses on.

But when the dew descended and faint stars appeared in
    sight,
All grew still, and Florence knew the men were quitting for
    the night.

Still she lingered in the twilight, hearing with a listless ear
All this, but waited, listened, for a sound she longed to hear.

Now he came, the handsome Walter, from the college just re-
    turned;
And she knew his step, and trembled, and her forehead flush-
    ed and burned.

But he greeted her so freely, with such frankness in his air,
And clasped her hand so warmly, that she knew no love was
    there.

Then her tender heart was broken, and she sank beside him
    there.—
It was summer in Dakota, and a stillness everywhere.

III.

It was autumn in Dakota; and the winds of autumn blew
Fiercely now, and rustled wildly where the yellow sunflowers
    grew.

All the air was dark and smoky; and the yellow straw would
    fly
On the winds; and corn leaves rustled; and a haze was in the
    sky.

Day by day the silent gulls would hover o'er the gliding plow,
Where the farm hand toiled and whistled, with the dust upon
    his brow.

Yet some days were calm and pleasant, when the golden-rod
    would bloom,
And the air was soft and laden with a nameless, faint per-
    fume.

Then upon the sunny hillside in the grass the herd boy lay
With his sleeping dog beside him; dreamed the autumn hours
    away.

He saw the small and fleecy clouds float through the far-off
    sky.
He heard the gopher's whistle and the plover's dreamful cry.

The cattle's tread was muffled, and his pony's champing
    seemed
Faint and distant; and he lay and watched the clouds, and
    yearned and dreamed.

Florence Lee was ill with fever; and she grew not well, but lay
Painlessly, and wasted slowly with the fever day by day.

Her fair sweet face grew hectic, and her breath grew short
      and faint.
She lay and smiled, or tried to smile, and uttered no com-
      plaint.

The doctor sat and held her hand and watched her hour by
      hour,
And wondered at the strange disease that baffled all his
      power.

Once he sat a long time silent; then he said, "Come, Florence
      dear,
Tell the old man all about it, for there's more than fever
      here."

Then the young eyes filled with tear-drops, like the old eyes,
      bent above;
And she told the simple story of her burning, useless love.

And so, she said, she longed to die and leave this world of
      pain.
For to die was better, better, than to live and love in vain.

Long he gazed upon the pillow where the golden tresses lay;
Then rose and dropped a tear and kissed the cheek and went
      his way.

Walter came one day in autumn when the sun was in the west,
And held her thin white hand and looked upon her peaceful
    rest.

Her mother and her brothers stood and watched, but knew
    not why
That smile was on her face and that new luster in her eye.

She told them she was happy now, and needed nothing more.
The gray birds chirped and flitted thro' the sun-flow'rs 'round
    the door.

The pensive lark was singing in the sunshine down beside
The garden; and her gentle eyes were closed; and so she died.

It was autumn in Dakota; and the winds of autumn crept
Softly now, and paused to whisper o'er the grave of her who
    slept.

And they came and told her story to a musing wanderer;
And he took his pen and wrote it. Read it, friend, and pity
    her.

PA AN' ME

Pa an' me, we had a fight
In a hay-cock other night.
I seen pa an' John the hired
Man a-restun cuz they's tired.

An' I 'es' sneaked up an' sat
On his stomick. Oh an' 'at
Made 'im grunt, an' right away
We was fightun in the hay.

'En I got to laffun so
I can't fight a tall. An' oh
Yes, a hay stuck into my
Eye, an' 'en I had to cry.

Pa an' me has lots of fun
In the summer time. An' one
Day mos' up to grampa's lake
Once we seen a rattle snake.

IN THE EVENING

In the evening when the perfumed winds of summer wander-
      ed by,
And the moon, a silver crescent, drifted down the western sky,
In the fragrant dreamful twilight sat two lovers, she and I.

On and on the fountain murmured with a musical, sweet
      sound.
Dreamfully the cries of children floated from the playing
      ground.
We heard the flitting swallows in the twilight darting 'round.

So we sat in blissful silence; and her cheek to mine was
      pressed;
And I felt her warm breath flowing on my lips; and felt her
      breast
Rise and fall with gentle cadence, as it lay on mine at rest.

Then began the old musician in the lonely tenement,
With his flute; and ah, the pensive sighs of melancholy, blent
With the syncopated breathings of the sobbing instrument.

For we knew the gentle master, why the mournful melody;
Knew his heart had once been buried far across the shining
      sea,

With his fair young wife, among the sunny slopes of Germany.

Then a sudden fear came o'er us, as the strain went floating
  by,
A dread thought we dared not utter: What if some day she
  or I?—
And we drew each other closer, daring not to whisper why.

HENRY

Now an old man lookin' back,
  I remember best of all
When I's jest a little boy
  How I'd hear my mother call
For me, standin' in the door
  Of the old house, when I'd be
Playin' 'round the garden patch
  Er the corn crib—"Hen-er-ee!"

Then when I was bigger too
  I'd be snarin' gophers, say,
Down along the dusty road,
  On a sunny summer day;
Huntin' hens' nests in the weeds,
  Er some other deviltry.
Clear an' sweet I'd hear that voice
  Callin' to me—"Hen-er-ee!"

In them days I recollect,
  Herdin' cattle fer away
From the old home, on a bright
  Lonesome afternoon I'd lay
Most asleep an' hear them sad
  Plovers cryin' over me;

Dream I heerd that fer-off voice
  Callin' to me—"Hen-er-ee."

Oh these feet has wundered fer
  Sence them airly days is past.
Mother's silunt many years
  Sence I heerd her call the last.
Yet a-roamin' on I hear
  In the nights a heavenly
Voice from sad an' fer-off stars
  Floatin' to me—"Hen-er-ee."

FOR HER

Amid the toilsome business of my life
    Ever I yearn for thee, for thee, my own;
    Whene'er I walk where frozen tree trunks groan,
With whirling snow and winter winds at strife;
Or where the night with summer song is rife,
    And yon pale moon looks downward from her throne,
    Ever I yearn for thee, for thee alone,
Ever for thee, my love, almost my wife.
Dearest, to dwell with thee were to rejoice;
    To roam with thee 'neath sunny southern skies;
    To hold thee to my heart when day is done;
To know no other music than thy voice;
    To wish no mirror but thy deep blue eyes;
    To feel no hand-clasp save thy velvet one.

ON HER ABSENCE

This night I think is very like the last,
   Save haply something colder, as I mind
   Her breath, scarce warmer than the laden wind.
But cooled my brow and cheek. Again the vast
And melancholy dome is overcast
   With multitudinous stars. Again behind
   The lonely spire I see the moon declined.
Again the wheat is waving where we passed.
And now she's gone, she's gone. While earth rejoices
   How shall I count the hours that creep so slow?
   How shall I tell the days that drag so long?
Where shall I list for hers among the voices?
   "Her voice was ever soft, gentle and low."
   Where shall I seek her face among the throng?

THE WATCHERS

On some brown hill the patient herd boy lies,
　　All through the dim and dull red autumn day,
　　Seeing the few clouds floating far and gray,
Seeing the mile-high plover soar and rise,
Hearing the cattle graze in muffled wise.
　　Now and anon his yearning glances stray
　　About the faint horizon far away,
Where the wide prairie meets the bending skies.
So, from their thousand homes of hopeless toil
　　Are longing looks of dull-eyed women sent,
　　Through weary days of work and nights of pain.
So, grim and wind-blown tillers of the soil
　　Gaze, and still gaze, yet find no solacement,
　　O'er their life's drear and limitless wide plain.

KING LEAR

Reading this book, as quickened fancy can
    I see 'tis midnight on a trackless, cold,
    And storm-swept heath. I see vast manifold
O'ertowering clouds the thund'rous heavens span.
By these red rapid flashes let me scan
    This shocked and shattered monarch, feeble, old,
    And tottering 'neath the kindless night—behold:
"A poor, infirm, weak, and despised old man."
When I am sick with rhymes of small account,
    Dull pithless verses, poems but in name,
    With what deep inward yearning do I pine
For thy rich leaves, O master paramount.
    Were all books else consigned to blasting flame
    The world were rich, methinks, possessing thine.

JOSEPH JEFFERSON

Is this an actor? and is that a stage?
    Tell us not so; we will not think it.   Here
    Behold the genial Rip himself appear.
Behold an aimless vagabond engage
The sympathy of thousands.   Let the sage
    Prate on; we'll rather love this quaint and queer
    Soft-hearted man, and drop our warmest tear
When he comes tottering home, infirm with age.
O gentle master of the mimic art,
    Thine is a people's love and gratefulness.
    Blest be thy days among us, long thy stay.
How fond a duty thine, to sway the heart!
    What shall we do when they are echoless,
    The halls where thy sweet voice is heard to-day?

ST. ANTHONY FALLS IN APRIL

Here at the falls I stand, while onward steal
   The last deep shades of evening. Speak no more
   Of the shut world. I only hear the pour
Of these stupendous waters, only feel
The plunging of these ponderous seas that reel
   And tumble headlong, jarring all the shore.
   Faint gleam the dim far city lights, while o'er
The gloomy bridge coach-freighted engines wheel.
Through weird and beckoning mists that rise I trace
The round and sinking moon. Upon my face
   Is dashed the cool spray, scented with the gore
Of upheaved rooted marshes. Ah the grace,
The wild tumultuous glory of this place.
   The multitudinous thunder of this roar.

WALT WHITMAN

Thou poet of the manly brawn and tan
    Of soldiership. Thou lover of young men.
    Thou wielder of the plane as of the pen.
Thou wanderer o'er thy country's plains, where ran
Her mighty streams. Thou good American.
    And now I read thy powerful Leaves again,
    Each with "its long, long history," and then
Proclaim to heaven, Here wrought an honest man.
Thou wert the champion of the sore oppressed;
    Of "those who've failed in aspiration vast."
    For poor and fallen ones thy bosom yearned.
Now after life's long toil art thou at rest.
    Joyful thou seek'st thy brighter home at last,
    "As soldier from an ended war return'd."

EDWIN BOOTH

WRITTEN IN WINTER'S "LIFE AND ART OF EDWIN BOOTH"

When I have read of those who living took
 Applause indeed from earth's admiring host
 I have observed the common lot of most.
And is't the same with thee? Hast thou forsook
Betimes all earthly glories? Do I look
 Vainly upon this picture? Speaks no ghost?
 Are thy vast honors, like an idle boast,
Shrunk to the compass of this little book?
O loved and gentle player, let this heart,
This trembling lip, these tear-dimmed eyes evince
 Thou art not gone indeed, but lingerest;
Or, wearied with the labors of thine art,
Sleepest like some tired youth. "Good night, sweet prince;
 And flights of angels sing thee to thy rest."

THE MOODS

I conned a poet's book from page to page,
    And marked the many moods in which he sung.
    And some were early songs, and bold, and rung
Of love and wine, and passion, and the rage
Of his wild violent heart. And some the sage
    Man-grown had writ; and here it seemed the tongue
    Of mighty genius free and curbless flung
Its priceless thoughts to men. But in old age,
In life's calm autumn free from pang or pain,
    O then his songs were sweetest to the ear.
    He sang of sunsets in the golden west;
Of yellow harvest moons, and gathered grain;
    Of heaven, and the hour we tarry here.
    I loved the tranquil songs of age the best.

IAMBIC PENTAMETER

Majestic cadence, plunging on and on
    Like the vast storm-heaved ocean, what sublime,
    What mighty utterances have thou and Time
Given to us! Since the poet's art begun
No measure hath had greater singers. One
    Of Florence journeyed hellward, and did climb
    To heaven's wide portals with thee. In thy prime
The mighty Shakespeare wrought with thee. Anon
The plowboy chants the Cotter's deathless song.
    A master weaves the tale of sweet Elaine.
    Beside the church, 'neath crimson evening skies,
The Elegy is writ. And all along
    The path of years they come, an endless train.
    Wondrous recorder, to have wrought this wise.

THE LEAVE-TAKING

As one on some late evening bids a slow
   And fond good-by with blessings manifold;
   Secures his cloak against the winter cold;
Sees for the last the cheerful embers glow;
Kisses the cheeks he nevermore shall know;
   Presses the hands he nevermore shall hold;—
   So I to-night take leave of all the old
Fond hopes, and forth a winter pilgrim go.
Farewell sweet visions, now a long farewell.
   The winds are raw, yet will I onward fare.
   The heavens are dark, yet will I brave the night.
Full many a snow-blown milepost I must tell.
   Then let them say, if I shall perish there,
   He that was poor yet strove as best he might.

THE FAIR ISLANDS

I think there be fair islands in the seas.
    'Round their bright shores the emerald ocean flows;
    And blushing lovers walk and woo in those.
I think there be unstoried Strophades;
And from their sunny sands no sailor flees,
    For there no harpies are; and there the rose
    Grows redder, and the lily whiter blows.
And often have I yearned to dwell in these.
But were I there I think in little time,
    As I should wander by the silver strand,
    My heart would languish with a deeper pain,
A fiercer longing for that far-off clime,
    Where the strong cattle roam the prairie land,
    And waves the wheat o'er all the golden plain.

THE VETERANS

I saw the war was finished; and the flags,
Soiled with the blood of heroes, torn with shells,
Black with the smoke of conflicts, all were furled.
I saw the camps forsook and silent, all,
Save when the feathered dwellers of the wood
Spilled sweet melodious music, and by night
The lean wolf prowled beside the silent stream.
The fields where battles raged were echoless.
Old cannon rusted by forgotten roads.

I saw departing hosts. I saw strong men
Weep, taking final leave of faithful comrades.
I saw each soldier sad, yet overjoyed:
All the old hardships, marches, battles done.
And home, and waiting wife, and peace ahead.

And had the weary soldiers peace at last?
I saw there was for them no peace in store.
Their fields were wasted by neglectful hands.
Their shops and mills corrosive Time had touched;
And o'er the silent forge and water wheel
The ivy and the lizard crept alike.

I saw the soldiers had but scanty thanks.
The dead were honored with cheap words of praise,
The living cheated of their sustenance.

I saw them turn again unto their toil
With that sweet patience only heroes know,
Take up their lifelong fight with greed and wrong.

O soldiers of the Union, not for you,
While ye do live to strive, will there be peace.
But for your comrades, sleeping without pain,
Sleeping on many a Southern battle land,
Sleeping where jasmine blossoms, and where rose,
Sleeping after their noble fight is fought,
Ah for your weary comrades there is peace.

A little while, and ye will follow them.
A little while, and we shall look in vain
For your worn faces 'mong the throngs of men.
A little while, and ye will be at peace.

O soldiers of the Union, lingering yet,
Walking a few more days with us who stay,
As one departing unto foreign lands
Walks yet a few more times among his fields,
Teach us the lesson of your loyalty,
That at the end, when ye are vanished quite,
When the last soldier's funeral bell is tolled,
The state may not want heroes utterly.

THE WIRES

O the wires! I've heerd the whizzin' of 'um buzzin' in my
　　ears,
Drivin' cattle past the railroad in them dim and airly years;
When the sun was bright in summer, and the gophers chirped,
　　an' birds,
The wires has promised things to me in queer and stirring
　　words.

O the wires! And take it evenings in the black and chilly
　　spring;
The wind southwest acrost the hills, I've heerd 'um hum and
　　sing,
Comin' home with pap from Hanks's, stumpin' 'long the ties
　　with him,
Neighbors' lights off 'crost the prairie, and our own light fer
　　an' dim.

In the war time too I mind the nights that follered, long and
　　still,
Me the youngest left with mother, dad an' Ike an' Uncle Bill
Gone together off with Sherman, how the wires would cry and
　　moan,
Bringing news of death to wives and mothers, weeping and
　　alone.

O the wires!   And now I wunder most an old man in the fall;
Winter winds and winter snowflakes, darkness comin' over
    all.
In the nights I wunder yit a-past the homes and cheerful fires
To the tracks, and stand and listen to the wild and wailing
    wires.

O the airly days that's vanished, that's "departed," as they
    say;
Father dead down south and mother north, and brothers past
    away.
Only me that's left, past forty, roamin' on an' harkin' still,
Tell I git the welcome message, an' go out acrost the hill.

THE REAPERS

Far toward the half-set sun I saw the reapers,
Near the wild ending of the wind-blown day,
Each driver with his four-in-hand, the horses
Hastening over the bloody-stubbled hills,
At one side and behind the warlike dust cloud
Following each: they were the charioteers,
Guiding over the shuddering fields of slaughter
Scythe-bearing chariots of the Persian king.
And now some turned the curve with high-raised whips
Like swords, and wide-mouthed prancing steeds: they were
The wild cloud-fighting warriors of the skies
The Romans saw o' nights i' the Punic War.
And still they passed in the red evening wind,
Far down the west in silver-shining dust,
Their reels flashing like burnished oars: they were
The Argonautic seekers of the fleece,
The fifty Greeks, sailing the sunset seas.

THEN DIE

First I shall roam the prairies high,
  The woods and rivers of my land,
  And walk beside the far sea sand,
Where wheel the gulls, and then I'll die.

O I must hear the evening cry
  Of loon upon the northern lake.
  O I must feel the ripples break
By southern bays, and then I'll die.

I will not chide thee, Death. I'll yield,
  When it is time, all willingly.
  I'll join the shifting dust. I'll be
Companion to the clodded field.

My time is all too brief to see
  And know the half that stays and charms.
  I have been taken up in arms
To view the passing pageantry.

I'll love awhile the wild blue sky,
  The mellow warming sun, the far
  And midnight moon, and each pale star
That swims the deep, and then I'll die.

DOANE ROBINSON

Down to Gary they's a man
Men don't mostly understan',
Jest becuz he's made of this
Here same stuff 'at Shakespeare is,
An' Jim Riley, an' the res'
Of them gifted men, I guess.

Queerest thing about this here
Robinson, he don't appear
Stilted up ner proud to me,
Like a poit ought to be.
Swappin' yarns an' walkin' 'roun'
Hilly streets of that ol' town
With a hay-seed freckle-face
Like I be.   Yet that's the case.

Some his poums seems to me
Jest as pure an' silvery
As the Lac Qui Parle that flows
Past the poit's house, an' those
Others makes me walk again
Dim red days in huskin', when
Mother lived, an' Ed an' Joe,
An' we wasn't scattered so.

An' I sez to him, as I
Shook hands with 'im fer good-by
After sundown, "Robinson
If I never see a one
Of the great men, dead er live,
Yet I'll always feel that I've
Held communion with one true
'Bard of nature', an' that's you."

ANALOGY

As I have trod the broad fields of harvest,
Where, far and near, clattered the sullen reapers,
And ever the hurrying shockers toiled,
And have observed the meek bewildered rabbit,
Scared from his covert, wandering through the maze of yel-
    low shocks,
Then tearfully have I thought
How in the wide world, estranged, misguided,
Wanders one I loved.

RETURNED

Dearest, I had thought to bring
   Honor to you when I came;
Not the loud and brazen ring,
   Not the sound of stilted fame;
   But a known and honored name
From the notes that I should sing.

To'rds an end that never nears
   I have trodden toilsome ways;
And at eve the rising tears,
   And at morn the longing gaze;
   And the hours have turned to days.
And the days are come to years.

After bootless journeying,
   I am come your hand to claim.
Nothing but myself I bring.
   I have sought an honored name;
   I have sung for modest fame;
But they would not hear me sing.

Yet I know in your dear eyes,
   Though I come with bayless brow.

I am welcome. Then arise;
    Let it go, I care not how.
    Poor hearts, dearest, long ere now
Loved and quickened in this wise.

Under far and bending skies
    We will journey on the same,
Where the wood birds sing and rise,
    Where the roses bud and flame.
    Let them keep their wealth and fame:
They may never know this prize.

SONG

In the fall, in the fall, in the foul weather,
  Black comes the night with wind and with rain.
Dim grow the black clouds, dim grow the bare trees;
  Bright glows the home light through the wet pane.

Where are the wanderers in the foul weather?
  Where are the drovers on the wild plain?
Where are the sailors, sailing the bleak seas?
  Where are the soldiers in the cold rain?

In the night, in the night, in the foul weather,
  Cold dash the driven drops on the black pane.
Bright gleams the lamplight; warm glows the fire light.
  Where are God's creatures in the wild rain?

GETTING HOME

A-sitting in this railroad car,
    That springs and sways and rips along,
I think of things which I have done;
    And some was right, and some was wrong.
For years, in these United States,
    I've worked amongst my feller men,
From Montreal to Mexico,
    And now I'm getting home again.

Oh many is the fields I've trod,
    The harvest fields of prairie states.
I've hugged a many farmers' girls
    By backdoor steps and pasture gates.
I've hoed tobacco in the south,
    I've been in Kansas, baling hay,
I've lumbered in the woods of Maine,
    I've oyster-fished in Ches'peake Bay.

I've worked in Texas, making ties,
    I've mined for coal in Tennessee.
And everywheres that I have went
    I've met with men the same as me:

Unlucky chaps that's had no chance,
   And so the devil's got us tight;
And yet we know what struggles is;
   We've had our tri'ls at doing right.

I know it's bad to drink and play,
   And take young girls and fool 'um so.
I've felt their hot and clinging lips;
   They'll hold and never let you go.
But us that's had our youthful hopes,
   And all them hopes is given up, ˙
Gits careless, as the feller says,
   An' drownds our sorro' in the cup.

You take a man that ain't no show,
   That's had no schooling, and is poor,
That's got to grind at common work,
   He's bound to go to thunder sure.
The railroads and the towns is built;
   The live stock trade is wilted flat;
The lumber camps is on the hog:
   What's left to make a living at?

Yet I'll git over this blue spell,
   And be a-joking first I know.
Oh some they is that's rich and great,
   But most of us has stayed below.
Oh I have worked at many jobs;
   Oh I have chummed with many men,
But I have lost 'um, here and there;
   And now I'm getting home again.

And now I'm getting home to stay,
   Most middle aged, with not a cent.
My mother's old, my father's dead,
   The chums I had they all have went.
The friends that lived, which I have known,
   Where is them scattered friends to-day?
The lonesome thoughts that rise in me
   I cannot tell, I cannot say.

SUGGESTION

Ain't you now on some cold bad winter day
Been readin' in an almanac, er say
Some old book, run acrost a little thing
'T'uld flash yer thoughts away to bloomin' spring?
Fer instance, "Summer days will come again"
Will make a person dream o' roses. Then
"In spring a young man's fancy lightly turns
To thoughts of love." Oh how a fello' yearns
Fer warm March winds an' disappearin' snow,
An' smiles of some dear girl he ust to know.

L' ENVOI

I have trod
A lonely herder o'er my native prairies,
On the tempestuous smoky days of autumn,
When a child:

And as a yearning student,
In dewy silences of summer midnights,
Hearing faint echoes from the antique poets
Across the wheat.

I have marked the seasons,
The coming and departing birds of passage,
The summer moon, the waning sun of autumn,
And the fierce storms.

What I have observed
In nature's round, and each pathetic message
Of the hoarse whispering south wind, I have written
In my book.

For it has told me
Stories of tender hearts, silent and broken,

Of ever dropping tears, and in the south land
The dead soldier.

And as the lover,
Wandering in the scented wood of Arden,
Hung his amorous poems on the branches
For one he loved.

So do I leave
My message unto them I love and honor.
The strong young men of now and of the seasons
Yet to be.

For they will come;
And they will walk these ways, and feel, as I feel.
Life's joy and rapture, and withal its sorrows
Acute and bitter.

Across the wheat!
O harvest toilers, soon the twilight deepens.
The Master waits, and the home lights are gleaming.
Across the wheat.